Quiet Desperation

Alfred C. Martino

Coles Street Publishing

Jersey City, New Jersey

Requests for permission to make copies of any part of the work
should be mailed to the following address: Permissions
Department,
Coles Street Publishing,
299 Eighth Street Unit 4L, Jersey City, NJ 07302
www.AlfredMartino.com
Library of Congress Cataloging-in-Publication Data
Martino, Alfred C.
Quiet Desperation / by Alfred C. Martino.
p. cm.
Summary: Marcus Cooper, a down-and-out former high school
football star, is offered a million dollars to cause a drunk driving
accident that will kill a famous comedian. [1. Thriller-Fiction. 2.
Entertainment Industry-Fiction. 3. Assassination-Fiction. 4. New
Jersey-Fiction.] I. Title. [Fic]- dc22 2011934850
ISBN 978-1-59316-833-9
Text set in Arial Unicode

Alfred C. Martino is the author of the award-winning novels, "Perfected By Girls," "Over The End Line," "Pinned," the stage play, Waiting For A Friend, and the short stories, "The Boy and Girl," "I Have Never Been Murdered," "Where Am I?" and "Breathing In Rio." Information about the author, and these titles in print, ebook, and audiobook formats, can be found at AlfredMartino.com.

Quiet Desperation

Alfred C. Martino

A million dollars...

The words rush through my mind, filling me with the kind of fevered thrill I only ever experienced throwing touchdowns on a varsity football field, two decades ago. Other times, the repugnance of what I will be paid to do weighs so heavily on me that I feel as if I'm caught in a whirlpool, struggling against the current, until I become exhausted and my soul is pulled down the swirling spiral.

Sweat trickles along my temples, eventually touching the corners of my mouth. The slight taste of salt returns me from these incessant mental battles to a dark motel room intermittently illuminated by the blinking red neon sign of the Valley Inn. On the night stand a telephone sits silently and, beside it, a lamp, faded Bible, and small clock.

It's 1:17 am.

Soon, I'll drive my Chevy east on county road 616 and, if all goes accordingly, meet Fate head-on. The thought dizzies me. Slowly, the room diffuses into a kaleidoscope of reddish shadows, while an ammonia smell stings my nostrils.

My life has been nondescript, if not insignificant. I have accomplished nothing of importance and have experienced little success beyond a high school gridiron. I am not, however, unintelligent. Yet my life has been mired in suffocating hopes and crushed dreams, and all the while the whole goddamn world is telling me what—and how much—I should have. And not to wallow in self-pity but as the cliché goes, if I didn't have bad luck, I'd have no fucking luck at all.

Fortunately, nothing lasts forever.

One night, a few months ago, marked the first time opportunity visited, and I was finally home. I took a break from my neighborhood dives and, instead, made my way into Manhattan. It'd been a long night of nothing-in-particular, but I didn't feel like crossing the Hudson back to Jersey just yet. After getting into a scrap with some Wall Street punks on Bleecker, I rode a cab to Live Bait, a favorite bar of mine on the East Side.

A haze of smoke rose to the ceiling, while Guns N' Roses blared from the sound system. I pushed through the crowd, passing by chain-smoking NYU students and a group of midtown hotshots tasting the spoils of their first disposable income. At the corner, a petite brunette sucked on her boyfriend's ear, as he casually shot a glance at an interested waitress. Beside them, a chick in a torn FIT sweatshirt, hanging fashionably off her shoulder, and another, dressed in studded black leather, flirted with each other then slipped into the bathroom together.

I sat at one end of the bar, turning my back to the droning conversations of an eclectic crowd keeping the night going after other places had closed. A barmaid in ripped jeans took my five-dollar bill and handed me another beer. When she walked back from the register I studied her pouty lips and *Penthouse* tits, covered partially by a white T-shirt, denim vest, and billowy auburn hair. Irish, I figured. Just beyond the dozens of arms, extended and impatient, she moved gracefully, sweeping down the bar to hand me my change. I thought about offering her the world.

Instead, I muttered, "Thanks."

Soon enough, a second, then third beer—and eighth of the night—had settled into my stomach. Though I sensed someone was standing behind me, I paid little attention, letting my thoughts drift. Over the speakers, Bono was singing and, for a time, I forgot about six grand lost on a sure thing at Monmouth Park, or being three months down in the rent. The music seeped into my body as I rode a wave of nicotine and alcohol, enjoying the solitude of my own little private Idaho.

After finishing the last of my Marlboros, I patted down my jacket and shirt pockets for another pack, but found nothing.

"Need a smoke?"

I turned.

The stranger was imposing: heavily-muscled, slicked black hair tied neatly in a pony-tail, tanned skin taut over chiseled cheekbones. He reached into the breast pocket of his charcoal suit and pulled out a gold cigarette holder.

I took one, put it to my mouth, and fired up. "Thanks."

"Worked with U2 when they first started out," the stranger said.

"That's real great," I muttered.

He stepped up to the bar uninvited. "The Edge is a prick."

My first time in Manhattan in months and now I had to be bothered by some asshole musclehead bragging about working with a band. I didn't have to read GQ to think his fancy suit and mirrored shoes were too contrived.

For a few minutes, the stranger did his best to force a conversation with me, and I did my best to brush him off. He'd ask a question or make a comment, and I'd offer a one- or two-word response.

"Look man," I said, finally. "I'd love to talk to you, but I don't wanna."

"Out on the town," he said, with a nod. "No need to be bothered, right?"

"Something like that," I said.

"I'll just finish this," he said, tilting back a seltzer.

"Whatever."

But the stranger didn't leave, and it pissed me all to hell. I had a sudden compulsion to stick my fist down his throat. I turned to size him up again.

Then something distracted me.

A Barbie blonde, straight off a South Beach postcard, swept through the front entrance and moved through the masses. In a sea of brunettes her hair was easy to follow, and it was obvious from her flawless tan that she hadn't spent much of the past few weeks within a thousand miles of East 23rd Street.

"Not bad," the stranger said.

She was more than that. Her self-importance was a noxious reminder of my bitch ex-girlfriend, Danielle. For two miserable years Danielle's voice was a constant rattle in my head reminding me that I was a loser, that I would always live a lonely, dirt-poor life. My jaw tightened and my fist clenched.

"Just some pussy," I said. "Dime a dozen." They all were.

The stranger grinned.

"She's begging for someone to set her free," he said.

I looked at him like he was full of shit.

But he just nodded. "She'd tell you if she wasn't so stoned. She'd say she needs a sugar daddy, a house in the Hamptons, a half-dozen platinum credit cards. What she really wants is freedom."

For some reason, I decided to play along.

"And that one?" I said, pointing toward a black chick sitting alone at the opposite end of the bar.

The stranger seemed to study her, then said, "Received some inopportune news today. She's debating whether to move back home. Indiana or Ohio, probably. But that would be a huge failure in her mind."

"You're a goddamn philosopher," I said.

"I watch people," the stranger said. "Watch their manners, their expressions, what they do. There anything you're especially good at?"

"Drinking beer."

The stranger smirked, but he wanted a real answer.

"Played football a while back," I said.

"Quarterback, right?"

I gave him a curious look.

"At your best, what was that like?" he asked.

"I had good field vision for my receivers," I said. "I could see them all at once, without really looking."

"That's what I'm talking about," the stranger said. "Me, I can read people, figure out what they want, what they need. Once I know that, then it becomes simple supply and demand. *Everyone* has a price."

"You're hardcore, man."

"What do you do?" the stranger asked.

"Not much right now."

"Let me buy you another beer," he said, waving a hundred-dollar bill to a suddenly attentive barmaid.

Soon enough, the stranger had me talking about the two things that gave me a hard-on—women and money—they were also the reasons why my life wasn't worth shit. As the empty bottles lined up, I could hear my Jersey accent get even more pronounced.

"...had this girl, ya know," I said. "Gave her the best I got, but that wasn't enough. Shit on me all the time. Until a right cross sent her crawlin' out the door."

He looked at me with unexpected interest.

I went on. "One night, I thought we were actually having a good time together. Threw down a fifth of JD and ended up in a parking lot in the back of my Chevy. I'm putting my pants back on—the sweat's not even dry—and she starts in with me. 'What kind of relationship is this? All we do is get drunk and screw.' I heard this shit too goddamn much. And she doesn't stop. 'Don't you get it?' she says. 'I'm almost thirty-five. I can't do this anymore.' So I tell her to hit the bricks. What'd I need her for anyway? 'Fuck you,' she yells. 'Just fuck you. You're always gonna be a loser.' I laugh at her. 'Go ahead and laugh, you bastard. I'm no whore. Why don't you go suck on your mother's tit some more?' The bitch actually said *that* to me."

The stranger shook his head.

"So the rage explodes inside me. Before I fuckin' realized I moved, she's smacked against the car door, her head's cracked the side window. My knuckle's red and she's bleeding from her mouth. Knocked out cold. For like a minute. So I lit up a cigarette and sat back."

The stranger nodded. "I know where you're coming from. I was screwed over by a girl…"

He told me his story. A compelling one. Seemed, as far as chicks were concerned, we weren't much different. Only later did I understand he made it up as he went along.

"…after two years she stole my Rolex, my two-year-old Rottie, then slept with my boss."

"Damn girl did that?" I said. "Did you teach her a lesson?"

"She learned," the stranger said.

For a few minutes, we just sat at the bar without speaking. The buzz of conversations and music became less noticeable, and I was getting weary from fatigue and alcohol.

"Do any work on the side?" the stranger asked.

I shrugged. "Why?"

"I'm putting something together right now," he said. "Easy work. Might need a driver."

I didn't say anything, taking a few swigs of my beer. But curiosity got the better of me. "Where?"

"You're interested?"

"Maybe."

"In Jersey."

"What'd I get out of it?"

The stranger smiled. "Cut right to the chase. I knew I was dealing with a smart guy."

I half-laughed. "Yeah, sure, that's what my high school diploma says."

"Diplomas mean nothing," he said. "It's about taking chances. Whether you're ready when opportunity knocks."

"I just want my share."

"So you'll seize the opportunity when it comes?"

"I've been fuckin' unlucky, that's all," I said. "With a little money..." my voice trailed off.

"Money is blood," the stranger said.

"Blood?"

"Shouldn't be green," he said. "It should be thick crimson. What can you do without it? Nothing. I've got a cherry-red Lamborghini Diablo prototype sitting out front, I'm wearing a two-thousand-dollar suit, I can buy any of these women. Know why? Because money is power. Little people worry about having 'just enough.' They waste their lives trying to make enough to eat, wear a few clothes, and have some hole in the wall to sleep in at night."

"I wouldn't mind a place I didn't have to share with roaches," I said. "Or a car that didn't suck."

"Maybe a Corvette?"

"That'd be a start."

"A hundred grand could—"

I stopped him. "Hundred grand?" If I was going to fantasize, I was going to do it in a big way. "Shit, how 'bout a million dollars?"

"Good," he said, as an odd smile snaked along his lips. "Very good."

I finished my beer.

"Like to look at models?" he said.

"No, I'm a faggot."

"Let's go then."

We left Live Bait.

I followed the stranger past the velvet rope of a club with a waiting line a block long. He moved with an arrogance that let every guy he shook hands with, and each chick who looked his way, know he had the world by the short hairs. We walked down two flights of stairs. At the end of a long, dim hallway, a bouncer stood guard at a private door.

"What's this, the inner sanctum?" I said.

The stranger smiled slightly. "Something like that."

We sat toward the back of the red-lighted room, in private, but surrounded by dozens of what looked like live mannequins— each one more exotic and willowy than the next. One of them brought me a beer. Then another. Then some shots.

And, all the while, the stranger and I talked.

"...so you think there's not much difference between us?" he said.

I nodded.

"Then if we dress you in an Armani suit, Bally shoes, slick back your hair, you'd be—"

"Just like you," I said. "Maybe."

"So where did things go wrong for you?" the stranger asked. "Or, better question, how do you make things go right from now on?"

I shook my head in frustration.

Some time passed.

Finally, I asked, "Serious about that work?"

"Absolutely."

"Guess my luck's turning."

"It's not luck, my friend," the stranger said. "I could tell right away you'd be the one for the job. I never had any doubts. I could tell you want the good things in life. You've got smarts. You've got desire. You just needed the opportunity."

I nodded.

"*Opportunity*," he repeated.

"Yeah, opportunity."

"So," the stranger said. "What's the difference between you and me?"

"Armani suit and Bally shoes," I answered. "Nothing else."

The next day came with a vengeance.

I woke up exhausted and hung over, my head in a haze. Alcohol had washed away most of the previous night. But I remembered enough.

On the floor of my place, among my dirty Levi's and balled-up shirt, I found a half-empty pack of Marlboros with a phone number scratched on the inside. I lit up and sat back, staring at the number, waiting. I wasn't sure why. I wasn't sure for what.

Eventually, it became dark outside.

Then it was late.

I made the call.

◆ ◆ ◆

The Trump Majestic, a forty-two-floor edifice of swank and exclusivity, stood at the edge of Weehawken's emerging waterfront, looming over the Hudson River. On one of the top floors, in a condo replete with all the excesses of an entertainment elite, Stone Redmond, naked, stared beyond the lights of the few boats and ferries out on the water this early in the morning toward Manhattan.

Beside him, on a king size bed, two women were in the throes of coke-induced sixty-nine. Stone grabbed a gold-plated Tiffany lighter. The flame's reflection danced in the bay window. In his other hand, he held a hundred-dollar bill. The flame lapped at the bottom of the bill until bursting across Ben Franklin's face.

"Too bad that asshole Koslov can't see this," he said. He looked over at the bed. "Cheyenne, you watching?"

A woman, her eyes hollow and sweaty cheeks streaked with eyeliner, raised her head from between the other's legs. "I'm...kinda...busy..." she said between breaths.

Stone pulled out another hundred-dollar bill and lit it. "Cum already," he said. "I want you to see this."

But the groans got louder and the writhing intensified, and soon Stone's patience came to an abrupt end. He tossed the burning paper on the bed.

"Send your little toy packing."

"Shit!" Cheyenne yelled, swatting away the embers.

"Now," Stone said, stepping out onto the balcony.

The other woman reached for Cheyenne. "Don't stop," she said, pulling her back down.

As much as Cheyenne wanted to continue, she didn't. Instead, she pushed the woman off the bed.

"Time to get out," she said.

"What?"

"Take your shit and leave. Now."

Hastily, the woman pulled up her leather skirt and zipped it, then slipped on her blouse. She grabbed her bra and panties, then, as she stormed out the condo door, said, "You two assholes deserve each other."

Cheyenne stumbled over to the dining table. On a mirror, she tapped out more of the white powder, nudged it with her finger into a makeshift line, then snorted it. She wiped her nose and licked her finger, then draped herself in a blanket and followed Stone out onto the balcony. She ducked underneath his arm and kissed him on his neck.

"It's cold out here, come back inside," she said. "I'm still wet. You can put the finishing touches on me. I'll watch your little bonfire after, I promise."

Stone was silent.

"Don't worry about Koslov," she said. "You did enough for him and that label." She touched Stone's forehead. "The creativity. The passion. The genius. It's all in here."

And still Stone said nothing.

◆ ◆ ◆

Four days later, the stranger and I met in Hoboken at the

Santa Fe Yacht Club, a low-rent bar across the street from the PATH station to Manhattan. Outside, fierce winds and bitter cold were unrelenting. Inside, the bar was warm, if not, comfortable. After two shots of JD, followed by a beer, my nerves eased.

At five o'clock—and not a minute later—the stranger approached from the back of the bar. Again, he was dressed to the nines. Not a wrinkle in his clothes, a hair out of place, or a smudge on his shoes. The stranger set a leather briefcase down, pulled off his overcoat and folded it neatly over a chair, then straightened the lapels of his pin-stripe suit. A waitress came over for drinks. I ordered a whiskey; he, a seltzer.

As the waitress walked away, the stranger said, in a low voice, "Marcus Cooper, glad you decided to—"

"Whoa," I said. "How the hell do you know my name?"

"We did a lot of talking the other night, Marcus," he said. "About the six grand you owe your bookie. And that crappy apartment of yours down by the Hollow."

I didn't remember mentioning either.

"This is bullshit," I said. "How do you know about me?"

"*How* is not important," the stranger said. "That I do, is what's important. Now that you know what I know, it'll make this even easier."

"Make what easier?"

"You said you were interested in work."

"And?"

"Are you?"

"Yeah," I said.

"I have a proposition for you," the stranger said.

"What do I have to do?"

"I need you to listen to everything I say."

I hesitated, but said, "Go on."

He began to outline the plan, specifying what would happen, where and how. When the part I would play became apparent, I said, "You're serious?"

"More serious than you could imagine," he said.

"No fucking way."

The stranger reached into his suit pocket. A page from the *Star Ledger* settled in front of me, yellow highlighter ink marked an article on the sentencing of a recent DWI fatality.

"It's New Jersey law, my friend. Only nine months in jail. *Only nine months*," he said, slowly and methodically.

I stepped back from the table. "You're fucking crazy. This plan is fucking crazy."

"Marcus," he hissed, through tight lips. "Didn't you tell me you could use a million dollars? To buy yourself a Vette, cash for top shelf pussy, your own place in the Poconos. Here's your chance. You're not going to let it pass you by, are you?"

"Not this way," I said. I knew he could see the confusion and fear on my face.

"So she was right?"

"Who was right?"

"Danielle," the stranger said. "She was right thinking you'd always be piss-poor and a loser?"

He knew just what to say.

"Here's a chance to spit in her face," the stranger said.

"But—"

"But what?"

He was making the whole goddamn idea sound plausible,

like it was just another job.

"Look, man," I said. "I've been in county jail enough times to know that I don't want to spend a goddamn minute in Rahway State."

"Rahway?" he laughed. "You'll be put in some minimum security detention center. It'll be like nine months at a country club."

"County club? Fuck you. Do it yourself."

The stranger stepped back.

"Relax, Marcus," he said. "Need a smoke?"

Reluctantly, I nodded.

"Here," he said, pulling the gold cigarette holder from his suit pocket. I noticed an engraved R.E.G. glint in the lights.

I took a drag on the cigarette, slow and deep. For a moment, it quelled my nerves. But, as a stream of smoke escaped from my nose, the stranger moved uncomfortably close.

"Look out there." He gestured toward the bar window. In the stream of exhausted commuters trudging by, one guy stood out, his weathered face pummeled by the driving wind. "Feel the despondency. He's worked ten, maybe fifteen, years at the same place. Bet he's got a cheating wife, a mortgage he can't handle. His life's worthless, you can see it. Every day he has to jerk his boss off. For what? Nothing. His life means nothing to anyone else, why should it mean something to him? Can you see it? Can you feel that?"

"I don't know," I said.

"Don't say 'I don't know.' If you can't see it in this guy—or any of them—then you're just as lost. You don't want a new life, you're waiting for this one to expire. Right here right now is a once-in-a-lifetime opportunity for you to change your pitiful life into one lined with hundred-dollar bills and women spreading their legs for you. They'll be so wet, you'll be able to sniff their pussy from across the room. Now, if you're content to piss this chance away, then don't waste any more of my time."

"You're asking me to—"

"That's just the means. Consider the reward."

"But I might die."

"Marcus," the stranger said. "Your life is dead now."

I turned away.

Outside, weary bodies continued past the bar. Their stoic faces reminded me of my mother and how for nineteen rotten years she survived on alcohol and valium living with my drunken pig of a father. All the nights she slept alone, while her family laughed. I knew it clawed at her dignity and stole her dreams, until she withered away into a shell of a woman. What justice it would've been to give her jewels and furs so that her petty, self-righteous sisters could choke with envy. Unfortunately, it was a year too late for her.

But it wasn't too late for me.

Before my conscience could react, I heard myself say, "Go over it again."

"You're ready?"

"Yeah."

The stranger smiled. "Good. Taste a little of the good life." He pushed a thick envelope across the table.

Inside were two packets of one-hundred dollar bills. My hand trembled as I stuffed the envelope in my coat. I had grown accustomed to my pockets being home to singles and fives, nothing more.

Then the stranger lifted his briefcase onto the table, released the latches on both sides, and discreetly opened the top. I felt my eyes widen, as I stared at stack upon stack of hundred-dollar bills.

Just as quickly, the stranger closed the top, reset the latches, and placed the briefcase back at his feet.

"It could all be yours," he said. "Now focus."

The stranger told me the job could happen at any time. I had to be ready. The plan was simple.

"Room 13 at the Valley Inn in Long Valley will be in your name," the stranger said. "Get there by midnight, a bottle of Jack Daniels will be on the nightstand."

The timing had to be precise, he made clear. There would only be a window of a half-minute to set the final action in motion.

"When I call," the stranger said. "You get on the road."

I nodded.

After my release, I should return to the motel, he told me. Pay for a room for two days.

"On the second morning there'll be a package with the rest of the money. At that point, your new life begins. Do you understand?"

I nodded again.

"And just in case you're tempted to back out, I know where you live, Marcus. And your sister, Louise, in Poughkeepsie—I understand your niece is quite the musical prodigy. I know a lot about you, and the people close to you. Everything, in fact. I'll be in touch soon enough to confirm what we talked about."

The stranger shook my hand, then he put on his overcoat and picked up his briefcase.

Before he left the bar, he gestured to me. "Remember, it's *your* time."

◆ ◆ ◆

Stone looked up. The building at 111 West 59th rose above the Manhattan skyline, dwarfing all other structures. He shrugged his leather jacket up his shoulders, then walked inside, catching an elevator to the penthouse floor.

"Good afternoon, Mr. Redmond," a receptionist offered in a pleasant, but serious, tone. "Have a seat." Behind her, two large oak doors stood boldly under the lettering, REQUIEM ENTERTAINMENT GROUP.

Stone sat down on one of the leather couches in the waiting area. Hold it together, he told himself, shuffling through a stack of industry magazines on a nearby coffee table. He had read too many times how he owed his career to Mikhail Koslov, the head of Requiem. Comedians just don't get that kind of support from their record labels, insiders said. Redmond must've made a deal with the devil. Either that, or Koslov thinks he sucks a good dick. It was all complete bullshit, Stone told anyone who would listen.

Not many did.

Koslov had the kind of confidence that slapped people in the face to make them sit up and take notice. Despite a pockmarked complexion and bald skull, his fierce eyes and penchant for Italian double-breasted suits gave him the air of a studied, if humorless, politician. He was physically imposing, with a thick frame that moved surprisingly well, and he had a razor-sharp business intellect. His demeanor was always professional, exposing his emotions infrequently, and, of course, his taste for intimidation was notorious. Early on, Stone admired these qualities in Koslov and, though he would now loathe to admit it, regarded him with a kind of reverence. This powerful man was going to make Stone big—seven-figures big.

And it happened.

During those initial lean years, Stone crisscrossed the Midwest doing second-rate comedy clubs in places like Traverse City, Michigan, and Wheeling, West Virginia. But then his career came to life with three raucous dates at the Comedy Cove just outside of Milwaukee—inadvertently recorded by a sound guy backstage—that people in the industry still talk about in mythical terms. *Redmond Exposed* would be released a few months later by Requiem. After a page-long bio in USA Today and a feature spot in *Rave*, Stone Redmond became the hottest comedy act on the club circuit, landing on the Billboard charts. A Vegas wedding with Cheyenne, the Victoria's Secret newest flavor, and an invitation to sit on Carson's couch after his first *The Tonight Show* set, would come right after.

As did news reports about round-the-clock coke parties and Cheyenne's Fifth Avenue buying sprees. Soon, Stone was attracting media attention for living a life that would make Jackie Collins blush—money to buy anything on a whim, relentless women just begging to swallow a piece of him, and power that could turn a monk into an egomaniac.

"Mr. Koslov will be with you in a moment," the receptionist said.

Stone nodded.

In a business where success and failure walk hand-in-hand, Stone's career quickly devolved into a cliché of highs and lows. And yet, despite the critics' lukewarm reaction to his third album and a well-documented month-long rehab at Hazelden, *Rolling Stone* put him on their front cover with the headline: "Dice Clay Takes On Redmond." Sales spiked, a recurring role on *Miami Vice* fell into his lap, and, with mercurial fortune, Stone believed he could again be at the top of the entertainment food chain.

"Mr. Koslov will see you now," the receptionist said.

Stone stood up, took a deep breath, then walked across the reception area into the vast space of Koslov's office. Gold and silver records from musicians of every genre and era were fixed in a meticulous pattern on the near wall, while a conference table stretched the length of a wall of floor-to-ceiling windows overlooking Central Park South. Koslov sat at one end, with a set of papers in front of him. He appeared calm, but menacing, his chin jutting out sharply from his jaw, his eyes seeming to relish the moment.

"Hope your drive in was a pleasant one," Koslov said.

"Yeah, sure," Stone said.

"Have a seat."

Reluctantly, Stone did.

"Would you like something to drink?"

"Let's get this shit over with."

"Yes," Koslov said. "You always were a bit impetuous."

He pushed the set of papers an arms-length away in Stone's direction.

"What's that?"

"Your contract with Requiem."

"Means nothing," Stone said, with a mocking laugh.

"Oh, no?"

"Not a goddamn thing."

"I beg to differ," Koslov said. "It means everything. No one just breaks their contract with Requiem."

"Mikhail, I've got an army of Jew lawyers who say differently," Stone said.

"Ah, yes," Koslov said, with a nod. "I believe they've been calling here."

"Then you know I'm as good as out of here," Stone said. "They've told me there are a few things to clear up. I can wait." Then he stared at Koslov. "This kills you, doesn't it? Really eats at you. Me, little Stone Redmond, leaving the mighty Requiem for Arista. It's not personal, it's business. They gave me a better offer. Four-album deal, HBO special, merchandising—all that shit."

"I would advise against this decision," Koslov said.

"Fuck you, Mikhail," Stone erupted.

"You forgot where you were five years ago."

"I don't forget."

"You were nothing," Koslov said. "We, at Requiem, took you in. We nurtured you and your career. We took some great risks, financially and otherwise. We gave you a future."

"I made a shitload of money for you," Stone said.

"We *spent* a lot of money on you."

Stone looked away, then, realizing he was conceding the truth, turned back. "I'm hot as hell right now. I've got magazines begging to do articles on me."

"Magazines..." Koslov smiled. "The *Rolling Stone* cover was a personal favor from Jann. And *People*? They'll do an article on anyone."

"I don't have to listen to this shit," Stone said.

"I suggest you do."

"I'm done. Gone."

"You have a contract to fulfill," Koslov said.

"I said, fuck the contract."

Stone reached across the table, grabbed the papers, and threw them at Koslov. They opened like a blossoming flower, slicing across his face. Koslov touched the corner of his left eye and drew back his hand. A drop of blood was smeared on his finger. He pulled a silk handkerchief from his suit pocket and dabbed the area.

"You're not going anywhere, Stone," Koslov said. "I *own* you."

Anger burst on Stone's face; veins on his neck surfaced. He leaned so far over the conference table that when he shouted, "No one owns me," the spit from his mouth sprayed on Koslov's rigid brow.

Again, Koslov dabbed his face with the handkerchief. "I'm disappointed that you choose to be combative," he said.

"Fuck you with that talk," Stone said, with a dismissive wave.

"It would be more appropriate for the two of us to come up with a solution that we can both live with," Koslov said. "That solution is, of course, for you to honor your contract."

Stone simply shook his head. "Here's my solution," he said, starting for the oak doors.

The blinking neon sign of the Valley Inn leaves a reddish hue on the wall of the dark motel room. I reach for a crushed pack of Marlboros from my shirt pocket and the nearly empty bottle of JD lying on the bed. I take a swig, then fumble for a cigarette—my last one. I put it between my lips and flick my lighter. It sprouts a flame that curls toward the cigarette as I suck in. After a moment, letting the nicotine fill my lungs again, smoke funnels out between my pursed lips.

I look over.

The clock on the night stand reads 1:37 am.

With a packed house still cheering, Stone winds his way through the Roadhouse backstage hallways to his dressing room; Cheyenne follows behind. Club employees, lesser comedians, and other hangers-on offer their congratulations for an incredible set, but Stone hardly acknowledges them.

"Stone, you were *so* funny," a woman says, stepping in front of him, a skin-tight dress barely containing her fleshy breasts.

"Think so?" he says, annoyed.

"Wanna help me put these back on?" the woman asks, holding open her purse.

Stone looks in, seeing a pair of white lace panties. He brushes the woman aside and glances back at Cheyenne.

"This might interest you."

Sweat beads on my forehead.

As the minutes tick by, the realization of what's ahead

focuses. I struggle to fight thoughts about getting the hell out of this motel room, driving my Chevy all night, to anywhere. Maybe up to Poughkeepsie. Pick up my sister and niece. We'd have to start a new life somewhere, but we could do it.

"With what?" I ask myself.

I've got nothing, I answer.

And that's when *a million dollars* dances in my head. Again. As it has every day and night since I met the stranger at Live Bait. I finish the bottle of JD. My stomach is warm and the semi-dark is comforting. No one to watch over me. I'm alone and that's the way I like it. That's the way I've learned to always like it.

In the dressing room, Stone rubs his forehead with his fingers. He looks up and stares into a mirror, seeing red veins streak across the aqua blue of his eyes throbbing in time with the beat of a steady headache.

"What time is it?" he asks.

Cheyenne looks at her Cartier. "After one-thirty."

"One more show," Stone mutters. "Then the lawyers say I can tell Koslov to go fuck himself." He lifts a suit bag over his shoulder. "Let's get out of here."

Stone leads them down another hallway to the Roadhouse back exit where he vaguely notices a large man, wearing a ponytail, seeming oddly out of place. As Stone approaches, the man pivots and offers his hand.

"Fantastic set tonight, Mr. Redmond," he says.

"Whoa," Stone snaps. "Back the fuck up."

"Just wanted to offer my congratulations," the man says.

Stone side-steps the man, before pushing through the door.

He and Cheyenne then cross the parking lot to the space where an attendant is watching over his black Porsche 911.

The telephone rings.

My stomach drops. I've felt that before. In the hours leading up to a big game, waiting in the locker room. I close my eyes. Stay tough, I tell myself. The phone rings again. I turn on the motel room lamp, and pick up the receiver.

"Ready?" I hear.

"Yeah."

"Time to go. Right now."

I hang up and grab my keys. I breathe in deeply and let reality filter into my body—it's game time. My movements have to be deliberate and focused. In a few minutes my new life will begin.

It'll be worth it...I'm sure.

Stone swings open the driver's door and slides into the leather seat, while Cheyenne gets in on the passenger side. He stretches out his legs, trying to loosen the stiffness in his thighs, then puts the key in the ignition and turns it. The 220-horsepower German engine rumbles.

"Make a right," Cheyenne says. "East."

Stone steps on the gas pedal, leaving a wake of swirling dust and debris against the red taillights, as the Porsche fishtails out of the Roadhouse parking lot.

I walk to my Chevy, and take a moment to look off in the distance at a section of 616 that lies below the ridge where the motel stands. I watch a solitary pair of headlights cut through the darkness, moving down the road another half-mile before a wide turn and sharp incline bring it back my way.

I get in my car and start the engine. I fasten the seatbelt and shoulder strap, then veer onto 616, leaving the blinking red neon light of the Valley Motel in my rear-view mirror.

Stone downshifts and redlines second gear, pushing the Porsche engine to its limit. A curve comes up. Stone needs every bit of the other lane, which he uses selfishly.

"Don't be an asshole," Cheyenne says. "Slow down."

But Stone ignores her. "The road's empty."

"I'm serious," yells Cheyenne. "Slow the fuck down!"

Divider lines pass under the Porsche frame in a continuous streak of white paint, as the road turns sharply in an incline to the right and then back to the left.

I grip the steering wheel.

The idea that time slows down at instances of tremendous pressure is a big lie. As I try to reach back barely a minute ago, I can't remember what the voice on the other line said—it's simply erased from my memory. I'm on an mission which part of my brain chooses to forget, even while it unfolds before me.

"Why're you doing this?" Cheyenne pleads.

The back wheels spin angrily as the Porsche hits a patch of gravel a few feet off the pavement and momentarily starts to slide. Stone regains control, then shifts into third gear and presses down on the gas.

"I'm indestructible!" he yells wildly.

How'd I become part of this? Who's in the other car? Questions shoot in and out of my head like fireworks, spitting out other questions, more hesitation, more confusion, until finally I slam my head into the steering wheel. The questions stop.

Less than a half-minute left...I figure.

Braking hard as the road sweeps left, Stone ignores slivers of light dancing on the trees ahead, a warning that another car is right around the bend.

I see the approaching car. My heart pounds to exhaustion. My throat hardens. No going back. The headlights grow larger.

And my mind eases.

"Oh, God—"

♦ ♦ ♦

I open my eyes.

And pull a blanket off my face. It's damp with what stinks like sweat. I look up. Cracks in the plaster draw a haphazard map on the room's ceiling. I turn over and dart my eyes toward the door expecting a black corrections guard to bang on the wall and shake me awake for roll call. But I'm alone. And there won't ever be roll call again.

Eleven days in ICU, another three weeks lying in a hospital bed, then two hundred and seventy-one days in Morris County

Jail. Now it's over. Freedom is only two days old, but it has an incredible taste all its own. A smile crawls along my mouth. When I think about what's ahead for me, my grin grows wider until I find myself beaming.

A shadow jumps along the window sill followed by three quick raps on the motel room door. I sit up. Boxer shorts climb up my scarred thigh, and an un-scuffed Air Jordan slips over my right foot. My pulse quickens. I grab my crutch and hop to the door. Reaching for the door knob, I'm certain I'm ready for my new life.

"Room 13?"

I'm momentarily confused.

"This is 13, right?"

I then realize the man at the door is from a delivery company. I nod and confirm my name. He hands me a briefcase-sized package and a receipt to sign.

"I only got one hand," I say.

"Sorry," he says, then glances down at my leg.

"Car accident," I say, knowing what he wants to ask.

"Must've been a bad one."

"I survived."

After scribbling my signature I step back into the room, lock the door, and place the package on the bed. I move to the window and close the blinds. For some time, I just stand there, staring at the package.

A million dollars...

The excitement of seeing and touching all that cash builds until I can't help but tear the package open. I pull off the top and sweep away pieces of Styrofoam until a compact disc box, with a small note attached, is visible.

My heart skips a beat.

"This must be a fucking joke."

I dump the rest of package and scramble feverishly through the wrapper and Styrofoam as if they're heinously hiding more.

"Where's the—?"

But nothing's there.

The room begins to contract. The cracked ceiling lowers; the stained walls close in. The smell of ammonia, now barely masking the rancid mildew and years of filth, fills my head. I fall to the floor and heave my guts.

Time passes.

Hours.

Slumped against the bed, I surrender to the truth.

"Mother," I whisper. "What have I done?"

The answer comes from Danielle as if she were standing in the doorway, with her familiar reminder, "You'll never make it. You're always gonna be a loser."

I crawl over and pick up the compact disc box. The album cover is a black-and-white backlit photograph of the comedian, Stone Redmond, on stage. The title, *Live At The Roadhouse*.

The handwritten note reads,

Marcus, Thanks For The Good Work